The Magic Set

The Magic Set

Written by Leslie McGuire

Illustrated by Kathy Mitchell

ISBN 1-887942-98-X

Contents

Special Words

Special words help make this story fun.
Your child may need help reading them.

dragon

house

magic

tree

wand

1. The Letter

When Billy Wibbly got up, it was windy and damp. It was winter. It did not look like a very good day to go out and play.

After having milk and eggs, he went to see if he had a letter. There in the box was a big one, just for him. It was a letter from Velvet Muttly.

When Velvet Muttly needed help, Billy fixed things for her. He helped her cut the grass. He fed her cats (there were ten of them), and things like that.

Here is what the letter said:

To Mister Billy Wibbly:
    Come for lunch at one o'clock!
I just got a magic set! It's big
and has lots of good tricks.
Just be here!

Your pal,
Miss Velvet Muttly

"A magic set!" gasped Billy. "I bet we can make a flag into a robin! If it's the big set, I bet we could make a rabbit hop out of a hat if we wanted to!"

"This is going to be so much fun," Billy said.

He ran back up the steps to his house. There was his dog Spot. Billy could tell that Spot wanted to do something fun, too.

Billy's dog Spot liked Velvet a lot. When Spot went to her house, she gave him cat snacks. The cats got upset when she did that, but Spot liked upsetting the cats.

Billy's mom was in the kitchen. "Can I go to Velvet's house?" Billy asked.

"Yes," said his mom, "but you need to make your bed."

"Please do the pots and pans in the sink. Put that junk on your desk in your closet, too. Just be back in time for supper."

Billy could not stop thinking about the magic set. He quickly fixed up his bed and his desk. But his closet was a big mess.

He finished the pots and pans, but he stacked them up in a very silly way.

He had a bath, but he forgot to put back his bath things.

He got dressed so fast he forgot to put on his socks.

Then Billy grabbed his jacket. He and Spot ran down the hill as fast as they could go.

2. The Magic Set

"Welcome!" Velvet said.

She looked a bit odd. She had on a frizzly red wig, lobster red lipstick, and big green glasses. She had on bell-bottom pants, a pink top with glittering moons on the front, and pink cat slippers.

All ten of her cats were sitting there. They had on sunglasses.

Her pet duck ran up to Billy. The duck had on a frilly pink bonnet. It said, "Come on in! Make it snappy!"

Billy stopped in his tracks. "I did not know ducks could talk."

"Oh yes," said Velvet. "She talks very well now. I tapped her with this magic wand. This magic set is the best!"

"Where did you get it?" asked Billy.

"Dad got it at an odd little magic shop," said Velvet.

"What do you want for lunch?" asked Velvet.

"I do not want lunch!" said Billy. "I want to see this magic set!"

"It's over there," said Velvet.

There, on the dresser, was a big black box. There was a big, odd-looking hat with grasshoppers on it, a wand, some red silk rags, a bunch of rubber bands, and some plastic rings.

"I think you will like the lunch I planned," said Velvet. "We are having lollipops and butterscotch muffins with gumdrops, mint pops, pumpkin ribbons, and fizz drinks."

"OK, OK," said Billy, "but what about the magic tricks?"

Velvet led him into the kitchen, saying, "Let's have lunch now, and then later we'll get to the magic kit."

The muffins were very good, and so was the rest of lunch.

"Do you think we can get a rabbit to hop out of a hat?" Billy asked.

"We can do a better trick than that," said Velvet. "It says so right here!"

Billy gasped. “How about doing a magic trick right now?”

“No problem,” said Velvet. She picked up the silly-looking hat with grasshoppers on it and began to mutter.

"Fobbly, dibbly, glop! Winking, dazzly, plop!" she said. "Mumps and bumps!"

Then she tapped Billy with the wand and yelled, "SHAZ-WOP!"

3. Uh-oh. Am I Stuck?

Billy felt odd. He felt his skin get tingly. His legs felt like stumps. His hands got fatter. He could not see very much, but what he could see looked red! Then he was bending over. All of a sudden…

...Billy began to huff! He puffed! He could not say things the way he wanted to. What was the matter? What had happened? He had whiskers! He was—oh no—a panther!

Billy began to shake all over.

"Good!" said Velvet, "but now I better send you to the right habitat. Tap six times when you want to come back. Do not forget!"

KA-PLOP!

The next thing Billy could see was a bunch of big trees. Water was dripping on him, and it was very hot. He could see bugs and frogs hopping in the bushes. Grasshoppers hopped all over him.

All of a sudden, he heard a thump in back of him. He ran up the next tree as fast as he could. But, when he looked down, he felt a bit sick. He grabbed onto the tree trunk. He did not like it up in the tree at all.

"This is not good. I do not want to be a panther," he said to himself.

So he tapped six times.

TAP! TAP! TAP! TAP! TAP! TAP!

FUZ-THUMP!

Billy was back in the kitchen, and he was not a panther.

"How was it?" asked Velvet.

"Not too good," said Billy. "I got way up a tree, and I did not like it up there. If you let me, I bet I could do a better trick than that."

"OK," said Velvet, and she handed the hat to Billy. "I think if you have the silk rag, the trick could be better."

Billy put on the hat and said, "What do you want to be?"

"I want to be a fish," said Velvet.

"That means I have to make you into a fish and put you in water, too," said Billy. "Hmm...water and fish, water and fish."

"Look it up in here," said Velvet.

Billy muttered,

"Illy, zilly, willy!
Bingit, bongit!
Zip-a-ding! ZAP-A-DING!"

All of a sudden, Velvet was standing in water! The cats began to hiss. They did not like being wet. They ran off.

But the duck swam by quacking, "Good job! I like this a lot better! Keep it like this!"

"I do not think I got it right yet," muttered Billy. He tapped Velvet with the wand and said,

"Zilly, willy, bongit!
Illy, milly, bingit!
Zip-a-ding! ZAP-A-DING!"

4. What Am I?

All of a sudden, Velvet felt as if she were in a big glass of water. The bottom was sand and mud and grasses and rocks. She looked up. The top was shimmering. She was under water!

Velvet felt things sticking out all over her chin! She blubbered. Then she flapped and said, "I know! I must have fins! I think I have whiskers, too. Did you make me into a panther, or am I a fish? If I am a panther, why am I under water?"

Then a big fish swam up to her.

"I am Codfish," he said. "You must be Magic Catfish! Please come with me. The crabs and the clams want to see you right now."

"Why?" asked Velvet.

"They have a problem," said Codfish. "We must rush!"

Velvet swam as fast as she could to catch up with Codfish. They got to a big ship. It was all rotten looking. It must have sunk.

It was filled with hundreds of clams and crabs. They looked very upset.

When she got up to the ship, the big clam began flapping his shell up and down.

"This ship needs to be a clam bed!" he yelled.

"No, no, no!" yapped the crabs. "We need the ship!"

"Tell us what to do," they all yelled. "You are Magic Catfish, so you must know!"

"I think you all need to be good," said Velvet. "Clams must not pester crabs, and crabs must not pester clams. You must share the ship, and the pond, too. Things are best when you share!"

The clams began to mutter, and the crabs stomped off to talk. They did not look as if they wanted to share at all. Velvet sat there. Codfish did not say a thing.

Then the big clam said, "We will do what you say, Magic Catfish, but we do not like the way the crabs do things."

Then the crabs flapped hundreds of little legs at him.

The big crab said, “If Magic Catfish says it is good to share, then it must be so. We will do it, too—but we still do not like the way the clams talk.”

“I think you will all be glad you did,” said Velvet. “Now I must go.”

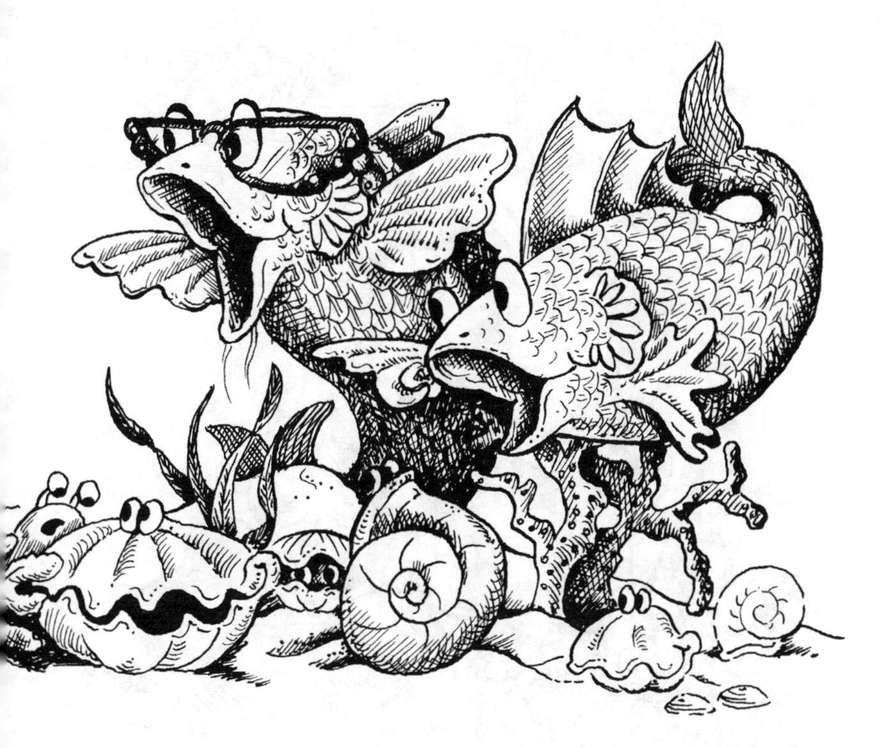

Codfish swam after her. "Do not go just yet," he yelled. "The frogs need to talk with you, too!"

"I have to go," Velvet yelled back, as she quickly tapped a rock six times with her fin.

TAP! TAP! TAP! TAP! TAP! TAP!

5. How to Get a Pet

All of a sudden, Velvet was flapping on the rug. Ten cats were looking at her.

"Put me back! Quick!" she blubbered. "I cannot be a catfish on a rug—not with all of these cats here!"

Billy tapped her with the wand and yelled, "Ibbly, bibbly, muttly! SHAZ-MAT!"

Velvet saw the cats getting littler and littler.

"Am I myself yet?" Velvet asked.

She could see by Billy's look, and how the cats looked at her, that she was not back to being herself.

Her skin felt odd. She felt big and hot.

"What am I?" she asked.

"You are a dragon!" said Billy as he and the cats backed up.

"Do not hiccup," he said.

"How come?" asked Velvet. "Why not? What will happen if I hiccup?"

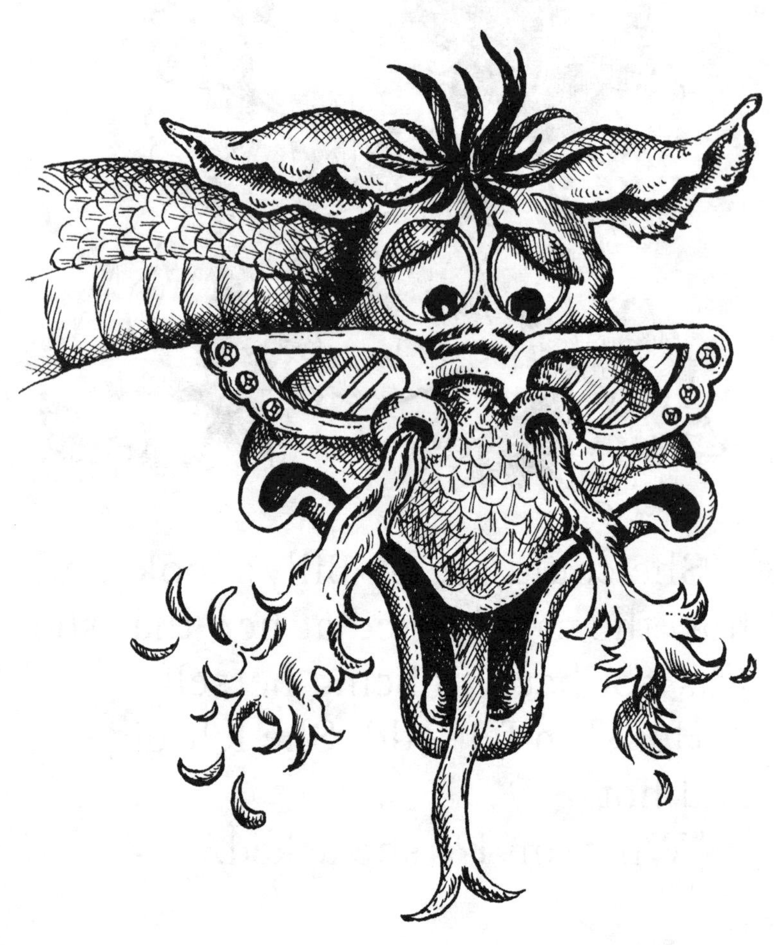

"Do not ask," he said. "You need to take a quick trip to Dragon Land. I will come with you."

Billy tapped himself with the wand. Then he tapped Velvet and said, "ISHKA BIBBLY! KAZZ-PLOP!"

All of a sudden, Billy was on a big rock at the top of a cliff. He was a dragon! Right next to him was a big dragon with big green glasses on. Thank goodness! It was Velvet.

Just then, a little dragon ran up the hill yelling, "Mom! Dad!"

"We are not your mom and dad," said Velvet.

But the little dragon grabbed onto her back leg and would not let go.

Velvet did not know what to do. She patted the little dragon and said, "It's OK. It's OK."

"My mom is not here!" he sobbed. "I want to go with you!"

“I do not know if we can bring you back with us,” said Billy.

“Please,” begged the little dragon.

So Billy said, “OK, just hang onto Velvet’s leg. No matter what happens, do not let go!”

Then Billy tapped Velvet and the little dragon with the wand and said, "Ibbly, bibbly, muttly, wibbly! SHAZ-MAT!"

Velvet felt a tugging on her leg, and then there was a big BANG.

There was a lot of yanking and tugging. Velvet did not know if the little dragon was still stuck to her leg or if she was still on the cliff with Billy.

Then they were standing in the kitchen. Billy was not a dragon! He was himself! Velvet was herself, too! But the little dragon was still hanging onto to her leg, saying, "Thank you, thank you!"

Velvet said, “I am so glad! What a good pet this little dragon will be!”

The cats all ran off. They were not very glad to see the dragon.

“Do dragons get big?” asked the duck from on top of the cabinet.

“Oh yes,” said Velvet. “They get very, VERY big.”

“This little dragon will be my pet,” said Velvet. “Billy, you can come and see him whenever you want.”

“Let’s call him Gumdrop,” said Velvet.

“That’s silly,” said the duck.

"Can I please have a muffin?" asked Gumdrop.

"Yes, you can!" said Velvet. "Billy will come to see you all of the time. We can grill hot dogs—with your help—and do lots of magic tricks, too!"

And that's just what they did!